T0123403

# The Ten-Year Year

**George Sanders**

WESTBOW
PRESS®
A DIVISION OF THOMAS NELSON
& ZONDERVAN

WestBow Press books may be ordered through booksellers or by contacting:

WestBow Press
A Division of Thomas Nelson & Zondervan
1663 Liberty Drive
Bloomington, IN 47403
www.westbowpress.com
1 (866) 928-1240

ISBN: 978-1-9736-5651-7 (sc)
ISBN: 978-1-9736-5652-4 (e)

Library of Congress Control Number: 2019902800

Print information available on the last page.

WestBow Press rev. date: 3/22/2019

I am an old man now, and each year seems to fly by. It has not always been that way. When I was a boy, the years seemed to last a long time, especially if I was waiting on something. This story is about one of those years. I was 9 years old and it seemed like it took ten years to turn 10.

# Contents

# The May Pole Dance

There I was, sitting in the shoe department of the Belk- Gallant department store in downtown Toccoa, Georgia. Every year, for as long as I could remember, my Aunt Mary would take me to town to get a new pair of tennis shoes for my birthday. Well, it was April 6, 1963, which meant I was 9 years old and finishing my third grade year at Big A Elementary School. Now, I did not normally enjoy going shopping for clothes, but I LOVED picking out my new pair of shoes. I was pretty fast anyway, but with my new shoes, I could fly. I could hardly wait to show them off to my friends at school. Much to my dismay, my friends were not nearly as excited about my new shoes as I was. My shoe show-off day really was just another day.

The school year was winding down with the usual end of year "stuff." Mrs. Dell was a good teacher, but I thought both she and I could survive just fine without seeing each other over the summer. I was starting to day dream about running and playing with my cousins and friends in our hillside neighborhood when Mrs. Dell brought me back to reality with a sharp, "Grady Farmer, you will be partnered with Rosemary Fitch." Whoa, what just happened? While I was daydreaming, Mrs. Dell had saddled me with Rosemary Fitch as my May Pole partner. You see, someone had the bright idea that it would be "cute" to have the 3$^{rd}$ grade classes perform a real May Pole dance. I didn't really know what a May Pole dance was, but I KNEW I did not want to be partnered with a girl for anything. Oh, Rosemary was nice enough, but she was a girl. Well, there was nothing to be done about it now. After all, how bad could it be? It turned out to be terrible! Not only did we have to practice during our recess, but we even had to hold hands. Did I tell you we had to skip also? Not a manly, running skip, but a silly, little, slow skip.

It took a few days, but I finally figured out the objective of the whole thing. You see, we had a telephone pole erected in the middle of our playground. It was about two thirds the height of a regular utility pole. Alternating yellow and red ribbons were attached to the top of the pole and the other end of the ribbons reached the ground with about 25 feet to spare. There was one ribbon for each student.

We formed an inner and outer circle around the pole. When the music started, we would begin skipping around the pole holding our ribbons in one hand and our partner's hand in the other. As we wound the ribbons around the top of the pole, the circles became smaller and smaller. After about three or four rounds, Mrs. Dell or Mrs. Jamison would blow their whistle again, and everyone would stop in their tracks and turn around. With another toot of the whistle, we would unwind the ribbons from the pole. Did I tell you I had to hold a girl's hand?

Once the ribbons were unwound around the pole, everyone dropped their partner's hand. The inner circle would turn and face the opposite direction. Another toot of the whistle would start everyone skipping, weaving in and out of each student we passed, until those strips of ribbon were transformed into a woven yellow and red cloth.

Boy, did we have a few tangled messes to start with. A lesser woman would have quit, but Mrs. Dell believed we could master it. We kept practicing, and believe it or not, that stupid May Pole dance turned out to be pretty cool. Heck, for some reason it even became kinda fun skipping with the girls.

The day of the performance finally arrived. Many parents and the rest of the school turned out for our May Pole dance. Our teachers told us to be on our best behavior because the first and second graders were looking at us as examples on how to act, and we needed to show the upper grades we were not silly or ill-mannered. Even though we had performed the whole thing to perfection at recess, it was a little different with everyone watching. Mrs. Dell said it was ok to have butterflies, and that they would go away when we actually started the dance.

Everything started out like clockwork. However, shortly after Mrs. Dell blew the third whistle to initiate the weaving process, Jimmy Johnson stumbled and fell. It looked like the whole thing might be lost.

Roy Reed, the tallest boy in class, caught Jimmy's ribbon as he was skipping to the outside. I was right behind Jimmy and caught the back of his shirt with my free hand and the seat of his pants with one of my new shoes. As if by magic, Jimmy popped up and cleanly grabbed his ribbon from Roy. Other than a little run to catch up, Jimmy made it back just in time to skip back to his place.

The rest of the event went smoothly and as the music stopped, we had our beautiful woven May Pole cloth. I happened to look at Mrs. Dell. A prouder look could not be found. It just occurred to me, teachers are just people, too. They worry and rejoice over little things just like kids. While they ARE human, they are different. How can they care about and believe in students like us? After all, we were the same folks who often made their lives miserable. I quickly lost that deep thought and realized summer vacation was finally here.

# The Cookout

The first days of summer vacation seem comforting: no worries and school seems years away. Right out of the blocks, you have a holiday, Memorial Day. My daddy was a World War II veteran and always made sure we paid proper respect, while also enjoying our freedoms fully. We always wore a small red flower, called a poppy, pinned on our shirts on Memorial Day.

This year we went to the courthouse for a remembrance service. A few short, patriotic speeches were made and the ceremony ended with the playing of taps and a 21 gun salute. I liked it all, but really wished I could have shot one of those rifles. After the soldiers walked away, I ran over to pick up the spent cartridges they left behind.

Daddy did not have to work at the thread mill on Memorial Day, but he still worked in his shop located behind the house. He could fix anything, and we often had three or four customer's cars in the yard waiting for him to fix. Even though Daddy was working in his shop today, he made sure he quit in plenty of time for us to get ready for our hillside cookout.

We lived at the top of the hill. Many of my relatives also lived on the hill. My cousins, Mitch and Tom, lived next door to me with their parents, Uncle Raymond and Aunt Belle. Uncle

Raymond worked with Coca Cola as a route delivery man and was always bringing home new products for us to try out. Aunt Belle worked at home and made the best tomato sandwiches in the world.

Next down the hill lived Uncle Tee and Aunt Beatrice along with their sons Jack and Billy. They had a shop, barn and pasture that we called the "4 Acres." They also had a good, rolling charcoal grill. Their house was where we were going to have our cookout. At the bottom of the hill lived Daddy's parents, Mama Millie and Granddaddy.

It was about 5:00 pm when everybody started arriving for the cook-out. All the kids were barefoot, sweaty and dirty from a hard day of playing outside. Even though I loved my new tennis shoes, I liked going barefoot better, and mama said it helped save my shoes for school when it started back.

Everyone had at least one dog. My sister, Ellen, and I had two dogs, Reni and Jip. The dogs knew which house to come home to for eating and sleeping, but the hill belonged to all the dogs and they were not about to miss a chance for grilled handouts.

Every family contributed something for the cookout. Uncle Tee had the grill, fresh hamburger meat and buns. Uncle Raymond brought in all kinds of Coke products in king-sized bottles. Mama brought in a gallon of fresh milk from her parent's farm across town. The fresh milk had natural cream at the top, and Mama knew how to make it into a great ice cream mix. Daddy and I had gone to the ice plant to get a big bag of crushed ice for the drinks and the ice cream churns.

The ice plant was a neat place to visit. Long blocks of ice had been frozen on large freezer rails. Men with large tongs and ice picks would bring out the ice. They would use the ice picks to make a perforated line around the whole block of ice at the desired length. With the tongs, the men would make a quick snap and the ice would break off along the prescribed point.

The men would bring the blocks of ice to the front porch where they would hose down the ice to get any dirt or wood splinters off. They would then put the ice on top of the crusher and place a large paper bag under the bottom chute. With a loud clatter and clack, the crusher would start chipping the ice into small chunks that would fall into the bag. On holidays and hot summer weekends, the ice plant was a busy place to be.

We brought the ice back and put about half of it in a big wash tub where Uncle Raymond had put the drinks. The rest of the ice was taken over to Grandaddy, who was in charge of churning the ice cream.

As Uncle Tee put his apron on and started grilling, the scrumptious smoke and aroma filled the hillside. He would apply generous amounts of salt and pepper to the raw burgers. As he turned the meat, he used a new paint brush to apply melted butter to further enhance the flavor.

We had been playing freeze tag when Uncle Tee called us up to eat. Daddy said the blessing, and everyone dug into the food. I started off with a hamburger and hotdog. I would have gotten more, but Mama made me stop so everyone would have an equal chance at the food. There were not only hamburgers and hotdogs, but all the chips, trimmings, and drinks you could handle.

We were about to pop when Grandaddy yelled out that the ice cream was ready. He had hand turned two churns of ice cream: one vanilla and one chocolate. Everyone got at least one cup of ice cream, but several of us got two.

After eating, the grownups started cleaning up, and us kids caught lightning bugs. I had a quart jar with enough fire flies to line the inside walls of the jar. I was going to use my jar as a lantern or night light in my bedroom. The funny thing about wild, brightly flashing lightning bugs, is that they quit blinking shortly after you capture them.

In the end, I just turned them all loose. Mama said they would be happier and would light up for us again the next night. I hated to do it, but I guess she was right.

Mama had washed the sheets that day and made me take a bath even though it was only Monday night. I have to admit the clean bed felt mighty good. My bed was pushed up against the wall and open window. I laid in bed with my left foot propped up in the window against the screen, catching whatever breeze might come by.

From my bed you could hear crickets and katydids but also the juke box from the Wig Wam drive-in and an occasional loud speaker from the drive-in movies down the road. On Saturday nights, I could hear the cars roaring at the race track and if the wind was blowing in our direction, the announcer would let us know who was winning. This night was pretty calm, and I was tired, so I went to sleep quietly reflecting on the day and wondering what adventures might be coming next. Good times!

# Water Jar Medicine

For some reason or another, all the moms on the hill felt like all us kids needed a good "cleaning out" at the beginning of every summer. While each mom agreed on the project, they had different methods of carrying out the process.

Each medicine had its own delivery system. Aunt Beatrice used a dark liquid that smelled almost good and tasted like some kind of spice flavoring. It didn't taste bad, but it sure wasn't good either. You just held your nose, swallowed a spoonful and it was over.

Aunt Belle on the other hand, took another route. This laxative used a minty flavored chewing gum to get the job done. You got the medicine in and you got to chew the gum to boot. This was actually a pretty good method.

Mama liked chocolate, so she gave us a piece of chocolate bar that was actually a laxative. This candy approach was very effective. Shoot, I would have eaten more if she had let me.

After the medicine was administered, each child was quarantined to their own house until the effects of the laxative wore off. During this time of isolation, I got the bright idea of creating my own medicine. There was an old stair-step flower pot shelf outside the house and plenty of used canning jars on the porch. Mama agreed to give me some old food coloring to make my medicine, and since it was just outside my house, she agreed to let me experiment with my project.

I had heard on the radio that "Doc" Tommy Scott was in town after touring the country with his "Old Time Medicine Show." He seemed to have made a good living selling his medicine, so maybe it had promise for me, too.

I lined the jars up on the steps and filled them with varying amounts of water. I then started dropping food coloring into the jars, making both base colors and an assortment of mixed colors. I figured I needed more than food coloring to make "medicine," so I started looking for other additives. I put a little garden soil in some, red dirt in others. Organic material such as worms and bug guts was added for potency. Grass, leaves, flowers and tree bark seemed logical as well.

For medicine to be used, it first had to be tested. Foot, even the FDA folks tested their medicine on live subjects. My dogs, Jip and Rini looked like they needed a good tonic. After all, all they were doing was just laying around in the shade sleeping most of the day.

The old saying, *"You can lead a horse to water, but you can't make it drink,"* seemed to apply to dogs as well. I tried spooning, pouring and rubbing my dogs with my concoctions

13

but they would barely even lick their noses. I finally left some good red "medicine" in their water bowl.

My "cleaning out" symptoms subsided later in the afternoon and I ran off to visit my cousins and check out their cleansing experiences. Mama called me up for supper and when I checked the water bowl, no significant amount of medicine had been lapped up.

At the supper table Daddy was talking about how Mr. Waters' poor ole dog had been poisoned and died. Seems like his

neighbor had rats in his barn and had put out some rat poison. Mr. Waters' dog had gotten into it by mistake. Well, I started thinking about the "medicine" I had put out for my dogs. I ran outside just in time to see Jip licking the bottom of the bowl. The only thing I could do now was to hope Jip survived. Mama called me in to get ready for bed. I went to bed, but could hardly sleep from worrying if I had poisoned my dogs.

The next morning, I slept in until about 7:30. It was Saturday, so Daddy had cooked sausage and eggs, and Mama had made some biscuits. After the blessing, Daddy said he had gone down to the mailbox and had seen a dead dog. Oh, no! I had killed Jip sure as the world. I started crying and confessing how I had made medicine and had put it out to test on my dogs.

Daddy said I should be careful about what I make and what I give my pets. He said he expected me to be more responsible next time. I was crushed! After a short crying spell, Daddy said,

> "I believe I will go get my shovel and bury the dog."

I said I would go with him and help with the deed. While we solemnly walked down the driveway, I couldn't help but feel more than terrible about the whole medicine experiment. When we got near the road, I saw the best thing I could have hoped for. Jip and Rini came running, jumping and playing toward us. Daddy just smiled and said,

> "I never said it was Jip or Rini that got hit by the car, but you still need to be more careful about what you do."

Whew! I hated it for the dead dog, but sure was glad it wasn't my dogs. I promised to be more careful with my pets and decided it was a pretty smart thing to ask my parents before I did anything I wasn't sure about.

# Vacation Bible School

Every year, soon after school was out for the summer, our church had Vacation Bible School. Kids from our church, other churches, school, and folks you had never even seen before came to VBS. VBS was more fun than regular church or school.

We would meet in the mornings at 8:30 for two weeks on the steps outside the church. Your grade level teachers would have you lined up and ready to march into the church sanctuary. Boys in the 5$^{th}$, 6$^{th}$, or 7$^{th}$ grade had the opportunity to carry the American or Christian flags. Girls in the same grades were selected to carry the Bible at the head of the procession.

After we marched in, we would stand up in front of our pews until Mrs. Jones played a few notes on the piano and then we all sat down. When it came time to say the pledge to the Bible and the flags, she would play a few more notes and we would all stand up. In just a few days we were like trained animals standing up and sitting down on cue. I looked forward to the day that I got to carry in a flag and have everyone stand up and say the pledge. I guess I would just have to wait a couple of years.

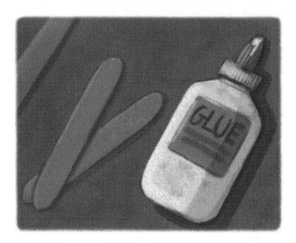

After the pledges, Mrs. Anderson would get up and tell us a story in line with our theme for Bible School. We would sing a few songs, and Mrs. Jones would play those magical notes, and everyone would stand up. This time, however, she would keep playing a song, and our teachers would lead us out of the sanctuary and to our classrooms.

In the classrooms, our teachers would tell us a Bible story or about a missionary in a foreign country. After each story, we would do some kind of activity to reinforce the story in case we missed the point the first time. I think the stories about Jacob, David and Jesus were my favorites. I liked hearing about the missionaries, but it was even better when they brought in a missionary from our church who lived in Liberia. He would tell amazing stories about the towns and villages he visited in Africa. Our church had bought him a motor scooter to get around on, and I could imagine riding a motor scooter through the jungle with lions and leopards chasing behind.

We would always have a mid-morning break. The moms were responsible for making sure we were well "snacked up" on Kool-Aid and cookies. Every once in a while, we would get fresh "Dixie Cream" donuts from the local bakery. I think I could have eaten a dozen of them without stopping.

When we finished our snacks, we would get to play some games or learn some new songs. We played tag, dodge ball and ping pong. My favorite was ping pong, and I raced to get to the table in time to play.

We ended the day with some kind of craft activity. It is unbelievable what you can build with popsicle sticks and white glue. That glue was amazing stuff. Just a drop on the end of one stick, stuck to another stick, would dry overnight so that the glue was stronger than the wood. My favorite thing to do—while the teacher was telling the story—was to sneak enough glue to cover the palm of my hand or the tip of my finger and let it dry. You could then peel it off carefully in one piece. Of course, we told the girls it was our skin, and they would squeal as they pretended to believe us.

After two weeks of VBS came commencement night. Moms and dads would come to church to see us march in. After the pledges, and the standing up and sitting down music, we would go to our classrooms with our parents.

The parents would kinda look at our work and help us collect our craft projects and take everything home. Funny thing was that the teachers looked about as happy about it being over as we were. I asked Daddy about that, and he said it was like banana pudding. It is really good, but you can get too much of it. I guess he was right. I had enjoyed it, but I was glad it was over.

# Rainy Days

When you think about summer break, you think about hot, sunny days playing baseball, going camping or swimming. You don't envision rain. Yes, you know it does rain, but it is hard to day dream about rainy days. You can't play your outside games or roam freely around the neighborhood. You just seem stuck!

The good thing about being 9 years old is that you can imagine just about anything. With a little effort, you can make bad weather situations good.

Every kid I knew wanted to be an astronaut. There was a new government agency to put men into space called NASA. There were only seven original astronauts being trained, and I was sure I could make the cut when I grew up. I had watched every Project Mercury launch on TV. I knew about the Redstone rockets of the sub orbital flights of Alan Shepard and Gus Grissom and the Atlas rockets of the orbital flights. Each mission was called something "7" because of the seven original astronauts.

My latest hero was Gordon Cooper. He had flown his "Faith 7" capsule around the world 22 times back in May to prove someone could survive a whole day in space. He was the first to have to use manual controls to get his space ship back into the Earth's atmosphere. He was also the last astronaut to fly in the Project Mercury program.

Today was a rainy day. I decided it was a good day to be an astronaut. Everyone knew astronauts laid back flat in their chairs on the launch pad. This was to help them survive the extreme "g-forces" they would have to endure during liftoff and reentry. I put my old football helmet on and went into the living room to the couch. Instead of sitting on the couch, I laid on the floor with my lower legs and feet resting on the seat cushions of the couch. I was now in position to blast off into space.

I started the count down, and every once in a while, I would have to respond to Control Central about the status of all the different systems,

> "Liquid oxygen, 'Go!' Thrusters, 'Go!' Cabin pressure, 'Go!'"

That means everything is ready and able to go into space. The much anticipated final 10 second count down was here,

> "10, 9, 8, 7, 6, 5, 4, 3, 2, 1, ignition...*lift off!*"

I could feel the power of the Atlas rocket shake the capsule off the ground. I could see the images on the ground getting smaller and smaller. I was headed for space.

We had a little difficulty in releasing the booster rocket, but I was able to manually release it to allow it to fall harmlessly back toward Earth. Before long, I was orbiting the Earth.

It was easy to move in the weightlessness of space. I could see the lights of the cities as I passed the dark side of the Earth. I thought I was going to break Gordon Cooper's record of 34 hours in space but then it hit me. I had to go to the bathroom. This is something I had not planned on, so I had to make an emergency reentry and recovery, just barely in time to make it to the bathroom. While in the bathroom, I thought there must be more to those space suits than meets the eye.

On other rainy days, my space flights lasted longer if "conditions" allowed it. Often times, I had to make repairs or save other astronauts who had gotten into trouble. On one long flight, I even nearly went down when my space capsule flooded on splash down like on Gus Grissom's "Liberty Bell 7" mission. On rainy days that suddenly turned pretty, I even had to abort the mission only to be resumed on another rainy day.

Rain may not be that much fun, but Mama said it made every thing grow and turn green. She said it was good for the garden. I guess that is so, but I know good rains also leave good puddles. I had a pair of rubber boots, and Mama would let me go to a low spot in the garden and play in the mud puddle.

You could pretend to get stuck in quick sand and nearly go under. You could make stick "boats" and bomb them with rocks or dirt clods. You could even dig canals to drain the "lake" and then build dams to prevent the drainage. As long as you had your imagination, the adventures were endless. Rainy days really don't have to be that bad at all.

# Vacation

D addy worked at the thread mill, and every August, the first two weeks were set aside for inventory and repairs at the mill. Except for a skeleton crew, everyone at the mill had to take their vacations during these two weeks.

I enjoyed vacation time. Daddy got his vacation check, which meant we had just a little extra money. When we went to the grocery store, Mama would let us pick out a toy from the toy rack. I had been eyeing a Snub Bee water pistol for some time, and with the vacation check, I knew she would let me have it.

As soon as I got home, I ran down the hill with my new water weapon to show Mitch. He already had a water gun, so we were all set. After a few battles and wet clothes, we went after other interests such as trying to shoot flies on the screen door. Aunt Belle wasn't wild about us shooting from outside the door into her living room, so we had to quit.

The first week of vacation was when Daddy would try to catch up on his car repair business and make some spending money. Much of his equipment was homemade. His air compressor was an old tank that had been welded tight. He had rebuilt an old compressor and mounted it onto the tank. Exposed fan belts turned the compressor with an old electric motor. It worked great. He could fix anything on a car or truck and even did paint and body work. I thought he could do anything.

The second week of vacation was the best. We loaded up in the old '54 Buick and headed for the mountains. Our first stop was Tallulah Gorge. It is one of the deepest gorges in the eastern United States. There was a "Stuckey's" store there, and Daddy would get a pecan log roll for everybody to nibble on.

Next on the stop was the ruby mine outside Franklin, NC. You could buy a bucket of dirt to sift through and hope you could find a ruby. They seemed to "salt" the buckets with quartz and an occasional tiger eye, so you would not go away empty-handed.

We would ride on up to Cherokee, NC and stop at the Indian Reservation. You could get your picture made with real Cherokee Indians dressed up in real Great Plains Indian attire standing next to a colorful tipi. It was fun in a touristy kind of way.

They usually had a few bears in cages. Some cages had a long tube running from outside the cage down to the bears. You could buy dry dog food and shoot it down the tube where the bears were waiting to eat. I thought this was kinda sad.

Daddy stopped the car at a station just outside the reservation near the Blue Ridge Parkway. I went inside to get some peanuts, and right inside the store was a wire wall with a bear named Otis behind it.

The man said Otis had been hit by a car when he was young and was about to be put down before the man nursed him back to health. The man said Otis would not survive in the wild because he had a bad leg and limped.

The sign said you could buy Otis a soft drink for a dollar, and he would drink it. I had saved $2.65 and knew dollars were

hard to come by, but I wanted to see Otis in action. Well, Daddy walked in to pay for the gas about that time and looked a little disappointed in me. I already had the drink open and the man grabbed it and gave it to Otis. Otis stood up with the bottle in his front paws and started guzzling it.

About half of it was spilling out, and the other half was going down the hatch. I looked at Daddy who could not help but laugh. I was relieved because he couldn't be too hard on me if he thought it was funny, too. I was debating on if it had been worth it, when Otis let out a bear-sized burp. At that point, I knew it was worth it, and to this day, it may have been the best dollar I ever spent on entertainment.

By this time, it was getting to be late in the afternoon. Mama had prepared a picnic lunch, and after a visit to Mingus Mill, we went up the Blue Ridge Parkway until we found a good picnic area.

Mama had water, tea, can cokes, and a can of chocolate drink for me. She even had a can of potato sticks for us to eat. We never got potato sticks, except on vacation. After eating our tomato sandwiches, it was getting a little late, so we headed home. Mama said Daddy didn't like to go to bed unless he was in the shadow of Currahee Mountain, which was only a few miles from our house.

Ellen had gone to 4-H camp earlier in the summer and told us a story she had learned about "Falling Rock." She said an Indian brave named "Falling Rock" fell in love with an Indian princess and wanted to marry her. Her father refused to allow it, so "Falling Rock" ran off into the mountains and started attacking anyone trying to go into the princess' village. It got so bad they had to put up signs to warn travelers about "Falling Rock." To this day, they have signs in the mountains that say, "Watch out for Falling Rock."

Well, after that unlikely tale, it started getting dark. Not long after that, I fell asleep and never remembered Daddy carrying me in or putting me to bed.

Our trip to the mountains and back in a day was our most common vacation, and I loved it. I guess there is something to the old saying that you need to "leave yourself wanting a little more." That way, you will always be ready to do it again. The only bad thing about our vacation was that it meant it was nearly time to go back to school.

# Back To School

When summer vacation began at the end of May, it seemed that it would last forever. Now, in August, the reality of school's return hit home. Even though I hated to admit it, I was excited for school to start back. New clothes and new supplies, coupled with the expectations of seeing my old friends and making new friends, excited me. All of those things, plus the anticipation of breaking in a new teacher added to the challenge of my upcoming fourth grade year.

Like I said before, the thread mill closed down the first two weeks of August, and Daddy made a little extra money from catching up on his car repair business. Other than the day trip to the mountains, the extra money went to buy new school clothes and supplies.

Ellen liked getting new clothes better than me, but Mama still made me go and try on my clothes. She would buy everything a size or two larger than I actually needed because she said I would grow into them. Blue jeans were rolled up at the cuffs anyway, so longer pant legs were just rolled up several times.

As you grew, the number of rolls was reduced to provide the desired length.

I didn't need shoes because I had mostly gone barefoot during the summer, and my tennis shoes were still in good shape. They would barely last until my birthday rolled around again next April.

After getting our clothes, we would go to Smith's Drug Store which had a great selection of school supplies. The big thing was a new loose leaf notebook. It had a cardboard base covered in light blue cloth. Mama would buy the large packs of notebook paper, and we would put several sheets between the sectional dividers and tabs. We would also get new pencils and sometimes a new ruler, protractor, or compass.

Most everyone had an old cigar box to put school supplies in. Those cigar boxes were supposed to hold needed supplies and were supposed to stay under your desk except when you needed something out of them. In reality, the boxes also housed favorite small toys or snacks and were being opened up much more often than the teacher wanted. There was a code of honor that went along with the cigar boxes. What was in the boxes was private, and everyone pretty much left everybody's cigar box alone.

When you bought your supplies, you could save the paper company's coupons for prizes. By cutting out the trademark from each notebook, pack of paper, pencil or whatever else they might sell, you could save points and pick out a prize from the paper company's catalog. The problem with this is that it took hundreds of points to get the smallest of items from the catalog. I usually lost my old points before I could add new ones to my total. Ron Ross was about the only one I knew who actually got something from the paper company. He was very smart and organized and didn't mind asking others for their unused points. I didn't mind because I knew I would never acquire enough points to "buy" the things I wanted from the catalog.

August 22, 1963 marked the beginning of a new school year. I walked down the driveway with my sister, Ellen, and our cousins, Mitch and Tom. Our dogs, Jip and Rini, also came down the hill to wait on Mr. Greene and his bus. As we got on the bus, I looked back and saw the dogs sitting on the bank, watching us ride off.

Everyone on the bus was quiet, but I knew that would change within a few days. We rolled down the road to the school, and I saw the sign, "Big A Elementary." Mr. Greene stopped on the side of the school parking lot, and all the elementary kids got off to go to our new classes. The older kids stayed on and rode to the high school. Mama had taken me to Miss Simpson's room during open house, so I knew where to go, but it was still a little scary going in the first day.

Miss Simpson was a comforting old teacher. She must have been at least forty years old. I felt pretty good about it, though, because one of my good friends, Anthony, was her nephew. I thought that should count for something.

Miss Simpson gave us math sheets while she assigned us to desks around the room. I had a secret that I was afraid would be revealed by the seating arrangement. I was very near-sighted and would have trouble keeping up if I had to sit in the back of the room. I was assigned the fourth seat back on the 2nd row from the right side of the room. This meant I could see some things written on the board on my side of the room but not much on the other side of the room. I was getting nervous about this arrangement when Miss Simpson placed my friend Rob right in front of me. Rob was a good, kind friend, and I knew I could get Rob to whisper what was on the far side board. Maybe my secret would be safe for another year.

Before I knew it, it was time for lunch. We had a great first day lunch: hotdogs, fries, slaw, apple sauce, and milk. Milk came in small waxed cardboard cartons, and you had to be

careful not to suck up a chunk of wax in your straw when drinking your milk. Several lunches were lost by swallowing a slug of wax.

Recess followed lunch, and for the first time, we got to go to the big kids' playground. Miss Simpson and Mrs. Algood divided the classes up into two lines, and we played "Red Rover."

The students in each line held hands tightly as they faced each other about 25 to 50 feet apart. Each person would get to call out a name from the other team who in turn would run toward and try to break through the hands of the other line.

When it was your turn to call a name, you would say,

> "Red Rover, Red Rover send 'Billy' right over."

If the runner broke through the line, they got to choose someone from the broken line to go back with them and join their team. If the line held the runner back, they had to stay with their new team. The line with the most members at the end of recess was declared the winner. It was great fun.

Before we knew it, the 3:15 bell sounded and we went to the auditorium until it was time to load up on Mr. Greene's bus. The first day had been fun and fast. As Mr. Greene stopped the bus at our driveway, one of the older kids got off the bus with a red flag to stop traffic while we crossed the road and headed up the driveway.

Waiting for us on the bank were our dogs, Jip and Rini. They looked pretty happy to see us, and almost everyday they would see us on and off the bus. I believed it was going to be a good year.

# A Fall to Remember

My school year was going well, but school is school, and there seemed to be more than enough work in it. Fall is an exciting time of year. Some of the boys were playing "pee wee football," but I was puny and kept tonsillitis, so Mama and Daddy would not let me play. Shoot, I didn't even get to go out for recess on cool days.

The air was getting cool, the leaves were turning colors, and Halloween was here. I dressed up like a hobo and went "trick-or-treating" in our hillside neighborhood. Each aunt, uncle or grandparent acted surprised to see us but was ready to give us plenty of apples, pecans, parched peanuts, and candy. Aunt Beatrice took holidays to a higher level and she never failed to go all out with goodies at Halloween.

Our neighborhood Halloween experience was great, but the school carnival was something even more exciting. It was held on the Saturday evening closest to Halloween. Classrooms were transformed into duck ponds and spook houses. They held dart games, bingo, and more.

The PTA cooked and served hotdogs in the lunchroom. My friend, Howie and I got to roam a little extra, playing and "spying" on folks because our moms were helping serve the food in the lunchroom. It was nice to be at school without having to worry about school work.

After Halloween, the weather started getting colder, and I started getting sick more often. For the past few years, it seemed I had to get a shot of penicillin every week or two during the winter. Dr. McKinley and I were getting way too familiar—in a painful way—for me.

It was Friday, November 22, 1963, and I had gotten a shot earlier in the week and was feeling pretty good. The day started off fairly normal. We had our spelling words to look up and define. We did a few multiplication tables, and read our "Weekly Readers" before heading to the lunchroom.

Because it was Friday, we had fish sticks for lunch. I didn't fully understand it, but it had something to do with our Catholic friends. It didn't matter to me because I liked the fish sticks and hush puppies anyway.

After lunch, we came back to our room. Miss Simpson had us conditioned to come back to the room and sit down whether she was with us or not. She was later than normal today, and when she did arrive she was crying. I had never seen a teacher cry before, so this must have been something big. As she composed herself, she told us President Kennedy had been shot while riding in a motorcade in Dallas, Texas.

Miss Simpson pulled in an old black and white TV strapped to a rolling cart. She rigged up a metal coat hanger as an antenna, and we all watched Walter Cronkite and his report on the shooting. Later that afternoon, Mr. Cronkite came back on the air and reported that the President had died. He took off his glasses, rubbed his eyes and just paused. I had never seen anything like this on television.

That Sunday, Mom was in the hospital with a kidney stone. Daddy took Ellen and me to see Mama. She had the neatest little TV mounted on an extension arm, so you could adjust how close or far away you wanted it while still lying in the bed.

I was ready to watch cartoons, but nothing but coverage of the assassination was on. A special bulletin broke in to tell us the accused assassin had been taken down while being transported from the courthouse.

The next Monday, we watched the funeral for the President. There was a riderless horse—with a boot turned backward in the stirrups—that followed President Kennedy's body being pulled on a horse drawn caisson. The President's son, John Jr., turned three years old that day, and when the President's casket came by, he saluted. They said hundreds of thousands of people attended the procession, and that the funeral was attended by leaders throughout the world. It seemed like a sad, sad time.

That Thursday was Thanksgiving. We sat down for a big meal at Mama's parents' farm. Nannie had wrung the neck of one of the chickens. After plucking the feathers off, she cut it up and fried it in a pan. The chicken we had been chasing around the yard earlier was now the main course for Thanksgiving dinner.

Papa Albert and Nannie Wallis lived on a farm, and instead of doing a lot of grocery shopping, they just gathered and worked up food from the farm. Freshly ground cornmeal was used to make cornbread and dressing. Sweet potatoes and pumpkins were used for pies. Fresh butter topped the cornbread and pies. Fresh, whole milk from Papa's cows was our beverage. Bacon and fatback were fried up from a butchered hog. Canned vegetables from the garden were prepared with just the right amount of seasoning. Everything was fresh and wholesome.

As we sat down to eat, Papa asked Daddy to say the blessing. Daddy started off like most blessings, thanking God for the food and for family, but then he paused a moment. Daddy had served on Saipan during World War II and was profoundly proud of our country. His voice broke just a little, then he said,

"Dear Lord, be with our nation during this time of sorrow and unrest. Lord, thank you for allowing us to live in the best nation in the history of mankind. Thank you for allowing our nation to survive these hardships because of the wisdom of our founding fathers to allow this nation of the people, for the people and by the people to be greater than any one person, even the president. Lord, be with the Kennedys, and help us to be somewhat worthy of the blessings you have given us. In Jesus name, Amen".

You know, even a silly 9 year old boy takes notice of sincere prayers. Those 6 days are still etched into my mind.

# Christmas

It seems like once Halloween comes, it is no time until Thanksgiving. When Thanksgiving arrives, you are on top of Christmas. For weeks, I had been looking at every page in the toy section of the Sears and Roebuck catalog. Daddy called it the "Wish Book" because it contained so many good things that nobody could ever get everything they wanted.

So that it did not overburden Santa, Daddy said I should limit my Christmas wish list to items that totaled $20 $^{00}$ or less. I didn't understand why they put prices on items in the catalog. After all, everyone knew Santa's elves made them for free. I guess it was as good of a way as any to keep us from getting greedy.

Even though I found lots of neat toys, what I really wanted was in the hunting section. It was a genuine 2-man "pup" tent. It was made of canvas and was water resistant, which meant as long as you did not touch the sides of the tent, and it did not rain too hard, you would probably stay fairly dry. It had a button down front screen and a floor sewed in to keep bugs and snakes out. It was really cool, but it cost $21 $^{95}$. I looked at the picture of the tent and daydreamed of camping out or playing army in my tent. The page with the tent on it got pretty worn and wrinkled.

Christmas Eve came, and I had to leave my list for Santa. The tent was too much to ask for, so I asked for a couple of metal trucks and some surprises in my letter. Mama got Daddy to read the Christmas story from Luke 2. They said it was important to remember the real reason for Christmas was about Jesus being born in a stable. It was hard, but I finally went to sleep after lots of tossing and turning. Mama and Daddy said Santa would not come until everyone was asleep. I think that only made it that much harder to go to sleep.

I woke up early to check out what Santa had left. Mama, Daddy and Ellen came in right behind me. Daddy suggested checking out our stockings first. I had a couple of good oranges, a tangerine, an apple, pecans and English walnuts.

Santa must have a lot of walnut trees because the only time we ever got English walnuts was at Christmas. I looked around the tree, beside the couch, and near the fireplace where I found a rectangular box. I couldn't read the letters on the box from across the room, but when I got close, I could see it said, "2-MAN TENT." Could it be that Santa knew what I had really wanted and left the tent for me? I tore open the box, and sure enough, it contained a real canvas 2-man pup tent just like what was in the wish book.

I could hardly wait to set it up, but it was a cold and rainy day, and with my tonsils, Mama said I could not set it up outside. I loved my tent, but if you can't play with your Christmas treat on Christmas day, it kinda dampens your spirit.

After breakfast, I hurried down the hill to see what my cousins had gotten for Christmas. Aunt Belle always had some goodies to eat and a sweet smile to go with them. Uncle Raymond would say, "Christmas gift" which was an old trick people would say to each other on Christmas to insinuate that you had to give them a Christmas present. It was just for fun because I don't think he ever got a present from us when he said it. Mitch and Tom usually had some kind of neat toy or game to play. This year they had a new carrom board and were playing carrom by flipping the rings with their fingers.

Mama, Daddy, and Ellen met me at Mitch and Tom's house, and after a short visit, we all would continue on down the hill to see Uncle Tee, Aunt Beatrice, Jack and Billy. Uncle Tee was a rascal and was always teasing us about something. Today, he was asking if I got hickory sticks and coal for Christmas, which he knew better than when he was asking. Aunt Beatrice provided even more goodies to eat and to take with us. Jack and Billy usually had some neat, new item just out.

After loading up on goodies, we headed on down to see Mama Mildred and Granddaddy. They did not have much but love to give, but they sure gave that out. Granddaddy always had juicy fruit chewing gum in his pocket, and was generous in giving it out. Mama Mildred had fixed potato candy and had a small box full for us. She made it by boiling a small Irish potato, which she mashed up. Next she added a dash of Watkins vanilla and mixed a whole box of powdered sugar in until it was the consistency of biscuit dough. After that she would roll it out flat, and spread peanut butter all over the potato slab. She then rolled it up like a pinwheel and sliced it with a knife. Boy, was it good!

Even though they did not have much, they made sure everyone had a present under their tree. Every year, I got either a pair of socks or a handkerchief. I have to admit their gifts were not always the ones I looked forward to the most, but, you know as I got older, I realized that the gifts of love and sacrifice are the best. As an old man, I remember their gifts as some of the best I ever received.

When we got back to our house at the top of the hill, we started getting ready to go to Papa Albert and Nannie Wallis' house for Christmas lunch. Papa and Nannie did not give many Christmas gifts but instead gave you things throughout the year whenever they had opportunities to give, like when they sold a bull or some produce from the garden. I have to admit I was a little down about not being able to play with my tent, but I tried being pleasant enough.

Papa and Daddy left to go to the barn. I didn't see them come back, but I did hear some loud banging on the front porch. I ran to see Daddy hammering a fence post nail through the stake holes of my tent into the wooden porch floor. He and Papa had set my tent up under the cover of the porch. This was better than I had hoped for. I could get in my tent without worrying about it or me getting wet. I even got to take my Christmas dinner inside the tent and eat it while I imagined being in some back country wilderness having to be quiet while hiding from bad guys or wild animals.

That evening, as we rode back home, Mama and Daddy talked about their Christmases as children. They said they would only get a stocking with stick candy, nuts and sometimes an orange or apple in them. That did not sound like much to me, but they seemed happy talking about it. I guess it really is not about how much you get but how you remember it. That night I crashed in the bed and was out like a light, dreaming about future tent adventures.

# The Sad Snow

I t seems everything builds up before Christmas, but the week after Christmas is somewhat anticlimactic. Christmas decorations start coming down. The beautifully wrapped packages turn into clumps of disenchanted trash that has to be disposed of. While all of this is true, you still have a full week of Christmas vacation from school to play with your new toys and to sleep in. Well, that is how it normally is, but my parents and Dr. McKinley had other plans for me.

Do you remember me saying I kept a case of tonsillitis for much of the year? Well, Mama and Daddy thought it was time for me to get my tonsils removed. Really, right in the middle of our Christmas break? They said it was a good time because I wouldn't have to miss school while I recuperated. They surely must have mistaken me for some other child that might mind missing a few extra days of school.

They also said I would be able to eat all the ice cream I wanted. How bad could it really be? You have the promise of feeling better and can eat ice cream to your heart's content.

It was a cold, cloudy morning when Mama and Daddy took me to the hospital. For some crazy reason, the first thing the

nurse asked me to do was to go to the bathroom and pee in a cup! I had never heard of the sort. I thought my tonsils were on the other end of things. Daddy assured me that it was ok, even if it did sound strange to me, so I filled up that little cup.

When I got back to my room, the nurse gave me a shot on the right side of my rump. The next thing I remembered, I was lying on a table looking at bright lights and a doctor with a mask covering his mouth and nose telling me I was going to be all right.

He asked me to start counting backwards from 100. I can only remember getting to 97 before waking up with the worst sore throat I had ever had.

Now, when all this started, the big promo was that I would get to eat all the ice cream I wanted. Well, guess what? I didn't want to eat ice cream or anything else for that matter, but they insisted that I at least hold ice chips in my mouth. This was no fun at all, and I could not look into the future far enough to determine whether or not it had been worth it.

Then the worst possible thing happened. It started snowing. Not just the few flurries we usually get, but a good steady snow. Before long the ground was covered. The nerve of it all. Everyone knew I LOVED snow! Here I was stuck in the hospital with a good window looking out at the snow and was not able to get out and play in it.

Mama thought I might feel better if I talked to Ellen, so she called her on the room phone. The phone rang and rang, no Ellen. She probably just had to go to the bathroom or something. We called again. Same thing three calls in a row. Then on the fourth call, Ellen, gasping for air, answered. She had been outside playing and sliding in the snow with our cousins and had not heard the phone ringing. Some sister she was. At the very least, if I could not enjoy the snow, surely she could stay inside and be miserable, too.

After a week of healing and mostly staying inside, I was ready to start back to school. I didn't realize it at the time but Mama said it became hard for me to fill up with food. From January until April, I gained 15 pounds and grew another three inches in height. When the other boys and girls got to go out for recess in "iffy" weather, I got to go, too. While I didn't enjoy getting my tonsils out and missing the snow, I sure was glad to feel better and I was looking forward to recess time again.

# Winter Doldrums

Just because of the cold, nasty, winter weather, you have to spend way too much time inside. School days seem long and hard. You get on the bus in the early dawn and by the time you get home, you only have a couple of hours of daylight to play outside. Because of the short daylight hours, you have to come up with other inside activities. Winter can be challenging.

One good thing about a tent is that it offers shelter for afternoon army games, camping adventures or good hangout places. You kind of feel like you are beating the elements by being able to stay outside longer than you would if you didn't have a tent. My cousin, Mitch and I had many such adventures.

My Daddy had built a shop in the back yard and had a good car repair business after he finished work at the thread mill. He encouraged me to hang out with him while he worked on cars. It was interesting but not really what you called fun. Daddy would pay me 50 cents a week to sweep up the shop when he finished a job.

For some reason, the winter days at school become mindless. In the fall, everyday is different. You are learning how to be in the fourth grade as well as learning new stuff, but by Christmas, you have already gotten all the school routines down. You pretty much know what each day and hour will bring. Then, the teachers go into hyperdrive with their lessons. You are hitting academic skills like at no other time because they are trying to make sure you learn all you can before the spring achievement tests. I hated to burst the teachers' bubble, but I don't think we cared nearly as much as they did about how well we performed on those standardized tests.

Late March came, and the time finally came for us to take the California Achievement Test. I wondered why in the world we were taking an achievement test from California. Most of us had never even been to California. Daddy said it was only because California had developed a test and Georgia had not. Anyway, all of a sudden, I was kind of glad Miss Simpson had worked us so hard in preparation for the test. It made you feel less anxious and really kind of eager to take the test and show off what you knew. Shoot, we were ready for whatever the CAT could throw at us.

It was kind of weird taking the test. It was like knowing some sort of secret code just to get started. Instead of just writing your name in a blank, you had to print each letter of your name in a block. Under each block, you had to "bubble in" a letter of the alphabet that matched the letter in the block. You even had to make sure you used a Number 2 pencil. Miss Simpson said we had to fully fill in the circle but make sure we didn't get out of the lines. Seemed like a long, complicated way to write anything out. I guessed all this must be part of the test, and if you could not figure out how to do it, you were pretty much lost.

I was getting a little bit nervous about the ordeal, but Miss Simpson assured us that it was just for the computer to read and was not part of the test. My friend Roy Reed had made a computer that could play chess out of a wooden board, a flashlight battery, some light bulbs, and a series of wires making circuits, and you did not have to bubble in anything. I thought those "smart" folks from California might need Roy to make a computer that could read names easier. Well, after a few days of testing, it was finally over, and everyone, even the teachers, seemed just a little more at ease.

# The Eye Ball

E very spring, after the all important testing was over, the teachers would loosen up a little, and allow us a few more recess opportunities. This year, someone had the idea of having a softball game between Miss Simpson's class and Mrs. Algood's class. Mr. Bowden, one of the sixth grade teachers, would be the umpire.

I was not too fired up over this event. I had never played Little League baseball. I was awkward and didn't fully understand the rules, but mainly, I could not see the ball when it was hit. My friend Rob was a good baseball player and had the best glove in the whole school. It was a black, pig skin glove that was big and soft. He could snag any ball within his reach. I figured since we had more than enough players to play the field, I would stand close to Rob who would look after anything hit our way. After all, Rob had carried me through two grades and was a good enough friend to have kept my eyesight secret safe.

Before you play a game of any importance, you probably need to practice first. Miss Simpson wasn't the greatest softball coach, so she allowed some of the Little League veterans to run the show. They chose the main team, which would field the regular positions, like the infield and the three outfield positions. The rest of us were told to spread out between the main outfielders. The only problem with this was that my sure-handed friend, Rob, was our first baseman.

Practice went well. While I did not catch any fly balls, I could use my speed to run down the balls that got through the first line of defense. My birthday shoes were getting pretty worn out by now, but were still good enough for hard running. Hitting was fine too. They only pitched the ball underhanded, so I could pick up the ball with my eyes quick enough to hit it. Maybe this was going to be fun after all.

Friday, the day of the game, finally arrived. At stake were 15 extra minutes of recess to the winning team. Mr. Bowden stood about five feet behind Bobby Albert, our pitcher. He called both balls and strikes as well as the bases. He even coached both teams when needed.

If somebody was having trouble hitting the ball, he would tell them how to stand and when to swing. If a good hitter was coming up, he would tell the outfield to back up. I thought this was pretty nice of him when he was helping us, but it bordered on cheating when he helped Mrs. Algood's class.

We were going to play for either an hour or five innings, whichever got there first. We were the home team, so we got to bat last. It was the bottom of the fourth inning, and we were down two runs and had a man on first and second base with two outs.

It was my bat. Mr. Bowden did not tell anybody to back up, but he didn't have to tell me how to stand to hit either. I fouled off the first pitch and then took two balls. I was beginning to think it might be my best bet not to swing and maybe walk. The next pitch was a strike, and I sure did not want to live down a strikeout, so I readied to hit the next pitch. It was low and outside. I swung the bat and hit a ground ball right at the second baseman. Running as hard as I could, I knew I could not outrun the throw, but Mike Iverson hurried his throw to first and threw it in the dirt. The first baseman could not dig it out, and the ball was headed toward the woods. I made it to second base, and the two baserunners ahead of me had scored. We were tied up.

Bud Ludsman was up next. He was one of our best hitters. It was getting close to an hour, so we knew this might be it. He got a good pitch, right down the middle. He gave a mighty swing and hit the longest ball of the game, but it was right at Matt Henley who made a great catch to end the inning.

Mr. Bowden liked softball and since it was still just under an hour of game time, convinced Mrs. Algood and Miss Simpson to let us play the last inning.

Vince Hill, the biggest, if not the tallest, boy in our grade, was up first for the Algood team. He had moved in from south Georgia and could really mash a ball. Mr. Bowden backed us all up. I was ready to run down anything that got through our main line of fielders. Vince swung really hard, but that was all I could tell about it. I was all set to react once the ball was in view. I was really far back trying to judge where the ball was by how the others were turning or running. Oh, no! They were turning toward me, so I started backing up to be able to run it down after it hit the ground. The ball never hit the ground, though. At least, it didn't hit the ground until it hit me in the head right above my right eye. The good thing was the ball bounced back toward second base after hitting me in the head. Vince, thinking he had a home run, was not running hard and ended up with a "heads up" single.

I looked around and saw Mr. Bowden and Miss Simpson coming out to see me. Blood was flowing down my face and gave me and the others a scare.

Mr. Bowden then sealed the deal.

He said, "Boy, didn't you see that ball coming?"
I sobbingly replied, "No sir."

To add insult to injury, since it was now over our hour time limit and the score was still tied, Mrs. Algood and Miss Simpson declared the game over, and everyone lined up to go in.

Mr. Bowden stayed back and took me to the office to call Mama. The funny thing about getting a cut on your head is that it bleeds really bad. The cut above my eye was very small, but it bled like a stuck pig. Mr. Bowden's wife knew Mama and Daddy, so he felt comfortable telling Mama about what I said about not seeing the ball coming, and suggested I get my eyes checked. What business of his was it anyway? I was good at faking about what I could see. I did not want glasses!

Mama decided to take Mr. Know-it-all Bowden's advice and set up an appointment with Dr. Fields. He was a nice old optometrist who was really neat. He first sat me in a chair that was in a long, narrow room. On the wall I was facing was a group of letters projected from what looked like a film strip projector.

He asked me to read the smallest line I could see. I could tell something was on some of the lines but the only line I could actually read just had one big "E" on it. He then put some sort of skinny binoculars up to my eyes. This device was on a metal frame and had a place for me to lay my chin in to keep my head steady. After clicking through a variety of different lens, I could even see the letters on the bottom line.

He did all kinds of comparisons and finally asked Mama into the room. He showed Mama what I could see without anything and what I could see with the right set of lenses. For some reason, my Mama cried right there in front of Dr. Fields. Away from home or church, I had never seen my Mama cry. I knew I had let her down by failing the eye test.

Mama talked to Dr. Fields about a payment plan to pay for my glasses. On the way home, I apologized to Mama about not being able to see very well. She cried again, and said she was so sorry that I was afraid to tell her or anyone else about not being able to see. She then smiled, and said her boy would have some glasses next week and would be able to see everything.

That next week was long in coming, and I still had not told anyone at school about getting glasses. I was afraid my friends would laugh at me, and that was about the worst possible thing in the world.

I went with Mama back to Dr. Field's office. The lady at the desk was very nice and called me over to a desk. She brought out my new, black rimmed glasses and put them on me for fitting. She had a small heater that heated the plastic ear pieces, and she bent them to fit nice and snug on my head.

She then took them back to Dr. Fields who called me into the room with the eye chart. I could read every line on the chart. He then asked me to read a sentence on a card about 12 to 18 inches away.

He said besides being near sighted, I also had astigmatism, so I had to wear bifocal glasses. This meant I looked through the top of my glasses for things at a distance and through the bottom for things close up. He said these type of glasses were common with older folks but not many kids had them. Great. Not only was I going to have to wear glasses, but I had to wear old man glasses.

On the way home, I forgot about all that stuff and was amazed to be able to see the bark and leaves on trees–not just the general shape and color. I was reading license plates on the cars ahead of us on the road. It was like I had a new super power. I could see things in detail. This was a good thing, but for some reason, Mama started crying again.

When I got home, I ran down to see Mitch to get his reaction to my new glasses. Aunt Belle must have told him not to laugh because he seemed happy and did not even comment about my glasses. The next day at school would be the real test, and to top it off, it was April 6th, my birthday.

# New Shoes

M ama made Ellen promise to make sure I wore my glasses at school. She didn't say anything about the bus, but Ellen thought it her duty to insist I wear them anyway. One of the high school students laughed and said,

"Look at ole four eyes."

I could have smacked him right in the mouth, but figured that wouldn't end well.

When I got to school, several folks just kind of stared at me as I walked down the hall toward the room, but they didn't say anything. I knew that wouldn't last long as I walked into Miss Simpson's room.

Mama must have tipped her off because I hadn't gotten in the room good until she said, "Why Grady Farmer, what good-looking glasses you have." I knew she didn't mean it because she had barely even seen the ugly things. Alan Howley started laughing and pointing at me until my friend

Rob stood up and just looked hard at him. Howley shut up quickly. I sat down in my desk and looked at the board for instructions. I could see them clearly and did not even have to ask Rob what they said. I think both me and Rob were kind of proud and relieved.

Other than catching people looking at me, the day went quite well. I liked seeing things I had not seen before, like the pictures on the wall or really seeing clouds. I would take my glasses off and then put them right back on. This seeing clearly thing just might be worth a few odd stares. We had other students who wore glasses and nobody seemed to bother them, and I guessed people would stop staring when they got used to seeing me in my new look. I liked being able to see things clearly!

During afternoon recess, Mama surprised me with cupcakes. She had cooked enough for everybody to have two. I know fourth grade is on the fringe of being too old for cupcake parties, but, heck, I don't think anybody minds cupcakes at any age. Miss Simpson called me up and everybody sang, "Happy Birthday" and then she gave me my birthday spanking. Everyone helped count the licks,

"1, 2, 3, 4, 5, 6, 7, 8, 9, 10," and then she gave one more to grow on. It was great!

Mama even checked me out of school about five minutes early to meet my Aunt Mary at Belk's shoe department. Sure enough, Aunt Mary took me on in, and Mama went home to finish my birthday cake. I had been looking forward to a new pair of shoes for a while now. This year, they had a new style of shoe that actually had rubber cleats on the bottom. I asked Aunt Mary if I could get them, and even though they cost a little bit more, she said yes. I put them on, and she paid for them.

On the ride home, I started thinking about all that had happened since my last pair of new shoes. So many good, bad, simple and profound events had happened since last year. I had grown in mind, body and spirit.

I had seen the pure pleasures and passion of ordinary life. I had seen our nation lose a leader and rebound from it. I had witnessed the strong adults in my life cry, pray and move on with life. I had prospects for a better life by having my tonsils removed and by getting glasses. I started to realize the importance of friends and of imagination. It seemed like it really had taken ten years for me to turn ten. I was finally in double digits! I wondered what adventures the next year had in store for me and my world.

# Acknowledgements

I would like to thank all my friends and relatives for giving me a great childhood. Your influence and love cannot be overstated.

Special thanks to:

My parents, Grady and Kathryn Sanders, for giving me a solid foundation so that, with God's help, I could handle life's ups and downs.

Raelyn, my granddaughter, and Katherine, my daughter in law, for being my editors.

Sylvia, my wife, for encouraging me to write even when I thought it was silly.

My sons Clint and Brett for being good listeners and advisors.

Blake, my son, for illustrating The Ten-Year Year and for keeping me on task.

Joanna, for formatting the book and getting it ready to print.

Printed in the United States
By Bookmasters